TONIGHT
AND
TOMORROW

TONIGHT
AND
TOMORROW

BY ROBIN BALLARD

Greenwillow Books, New York

FOR MY MOM

Pen and ink and watercolors were used for the full-color art. The text type is Futura. Copyright © 2000 by Robin Ballard. All rights reserved.
No part of this book may be reproduced or utilized in any form or by any means, electronic or mechanical, including photocopying, recording, or
by any information storage and retrieval system, without permission in writing from the Publisher, Greenwillow Books, a division of William Morrow
& Company, Inc., 1350 Avenue of the Americas, New York, NY 10019. www.williammorrow.com Printed in Hong Kong by South China Printing
Company (1988) Ltd. First Edition 10 9 8 7 6 5 4 3 2 1
Library of Congress Cataloging-in-Publication Data: Ballard, Robin. Tonight and tomorrow / by Robin Ballard. p. cm.
Summary: At night as he prepares for bed, a young boy describes different things in his room and what he will do with them tomorrow.
ISBN 0-688-16790-X [1. Bedtime—Fiction.] I. Title. PZ7.B2125To 2000 [E]—dc21 98-50789 CIP AC

It is night. And in the night stands a house.

And in the house is a room. It is my room.

A tiny night-light shines in the corner, just bright enough for me to see. Tomorrow when I get up, my room will be filled with light.

Next to my night-light there is a window.

At night it's full of shadows, but tomorrow

I will open the curtains and see what the

day is like.

In the other corner is a chest of drawers
full of my clothes. Tomorrow I will pull out
underwear and a pair of pants, a shirt,
and two socks to wear.

My heavy backpack is on the table. Inside
is a book, some paper, a pencil case, and
room enough for my lunch. Tomorrow I will
go to school.

Next to the lamp is a photo in a frame.

It is a picture of my best friend, Joe.

Tomorrow we will play together until

it's time to go home.

In a chest are some toys, but more are on the floor. Later in the afternoon I will build a palace made from old cardboard boxes.

Our cat is curled up on the stool. She is

dreaming and twitching her whiskers.

Tomorrow she will come to me, hungry

for her dinner.

SAM

On the shelves above my bed are some
books. Tomorrow night after my bath,
I will choose a story and Mommy will
read it to me.

Now I close my eyes.

The sooner I go to sleep, the sooner tomorrow will be here!

Good night.